T0368455

Skier Safety
with
Bo and Dacious

Written and Illustrated by
Rey Brooke

Balboa Press books may be ordered through booksellers or by contacting:

Balboa Press
A Division of Hay House
1663 Liberty Drive
Bloomington, IN 47403
www.balboapress.com
844-682-1282

ISBN: 979-8-7652-5679-4 (sc)
979-8-7652-5678-7 (e)

Library of Congress Control Number: 2024922522

Print information available on the last page.

Balboa Press rev. date: 10/28/2024

BALBOA.PRESS
A DIVISION OF HAY HOUSE

Dedicated to:

My son Bodhi; May you find the same thrill and inspiration from the high country that I do. That of course is second to the thrill and inspiration I get from being your Dad! May you be a man of the mountains and a mountain of a man. I love you son!

In memory of Andre Heartlief

In the mountains just west of the great divide. A cool breeze shivers through the trees, snow is falling and bounding with excitement we can't wait to get back on skis.

My Name is Dacious, I'm an Avalanche Dog!

Bo here's my trainer and the coolest guy I know.

We make a good team!

Keeping people safe, playing in the snow
Ahhhhh living the dream!

We rise before the sun, stretch out our muscles nice and slow.

Get ready for work. Yelp yelp!! Weatherman's calling for more snow!

We drink plenty of water and fill
up our bellies to perform our best.

We work hard, wake up early, so
we make sure to get plenty of rest.

I have a fur coat, so all I wear is my vest and a smile, but my human friend Bo needs his:

Thermals   Goggles
Snow jacket   Gloves
Snow pants   Warm socks.
Helmet

Wait a minute! Where are my socks!

He He!! It takes him a while.

We're out the door not skipping a beat.
The air is fresh and the snow squeaks beneath our feet.

We watch the sunrise riding first chair,
thinking of our favorite powder stash,
hope no one beats us there!

After openings and work that needs doing Bo likes to have a coffee and gives me some pats.

Then back to work. This is no job for cats!

On blue bird days you can get burnt from the sun.
We wear plenty of sunscreen cause getting burnt
is no fun.

We got each others back, I ski with my buddy.

I look after Bo and he looks after me.

If we happen to get separated we have a meeting place, so he knows where I'll be.

If you need our help get injured, or lost.
We'll be there in a flash! Get our attention,
by putting your skis up hill of you and Crossed.

Make a plan and look before you leap. Play it smart!

Think about your

speed,
approach,
takeoff,
maneuver
and landing

Before you start!

Skiing in avalanche terrain is DANGEROUS!

But if you're going to do it bring a buddy and the right equipment.

Beacon,
shovel,
probe
and know how to use it!

Know the Code! Observe warnings and signs.
Skiing reckless, or outside your ability you
could have a bad time.

Expect the unexpected. Changing weather and Conditions. Head on a swivel looking for:

Bare spots
Rocks Stumps
Trees
and Collisions

Powder days are our favorite!!

I get so excited I can't stop wagging my tail!

Bo and I laugh and hooowwwwlll all the way down the ski trail!

The view from our office is GREAT!

Looking out over the range and our sleepy little town.

Seeing the Sunrises in the mornings and each night at sweeps watching the alpenglow of the sun going down.

The End

Woof Woof!

Powder Day

Verse 1

There's a storm coming in

The weatherman says snow

and so Im up in the morning
before the sun can rise

you might be asking to yourself why

Verse 2

I'm drinking a cup of coffee

Walking to the lift

It's good and hot with sugar and cream

The snow is even better than
what I saw in my dreams

Verse 3

I got this tune

Stuck in my head

While I'm laying down a sweet little zipper track

Hiking up the bowls i got the wind to my back

Chorus

Cause it's a powder day

18 inches, still falling heading out to play

ooooh yeah its a powder day

Its steep and deep weaving through the trees

Hey yeah its a powder day

It feels like you're flying and
cuts like warm butter

ooooh yeah its a powder day

hey yeah its a powder day

Printed in the United States
by Baker & Taylor Publisher Services